WITCH OR PRINCESS?

"Let's hear what some of you are wearing for Halloween," Mrs. Otis asked at the beginning of class.

"I'm going to be a genie," Caroline said. "With pointy shoes and a veil."

"And I'm going to be a tooth fairy," Lois added.

Elizabeth hoped Mrs. Otis wouldn't call on her. She and Jessica still hadn't decided who would wear the witch costume and who would wear the princess costume.

But Mrs. Otis didn't call on Elizabeth. She called on Jessica. "What's your costume going to be?" she asked.

"A princess," Jessica answered quickly.

Elizabeth stared at her sister. "Jessica," she whispered. "That's not fair! I want to be the princess, too."

Bantam Skylark Books in the
SWEET VALLEY KIDS series
Ask your bookseller for the
books you have missed

SWEET VALLEY KIDS

SWEET VALLEY TRICK OR TREAT

Written by
Molly Mia Stewart

Created by
FRANCINE PASCAL

Illustrated by
Ying-Hwa Hu

A BANTAM SKYLARK BOOK®
NEW YORK · TORONTO · LONDON · SYDNEY · AUCKLAND

RL 2, 005–008

SWEET VALLEY TRICK OR TREAT
A Bantam Skylark Book / October 1990

Sweet Valley High and *Sweet Valley Kids are
trademarks of Francine Pascal.*

Conceived by Francine Pascal

*Produced by Daniel Weiss Associates, Inc.
33 West 17th Street
New York, NY 10011*

Cover art by Susan Tang

Interior illustrations by Ying-Hwa Hu

*Skylark Books is a registered trademark of Bantam Books, a division of
Bantam Doubleday Dell Publishing Group, Inc.*

ISBN 0-553-15825-2

Published simultaneously in the United States and Canada

*Bantam Books are published by Bantam Books, a division of Bantam
Doubleday Dell Publishing Group, Inc. Its trademark, consisting of the
words "Bantam Books" and the portrayal of a rooster, is Registered in U.S.
Patent and Trademark Office and in other countries. Marca Registrada.
Bantam Books, 666 Fifth Avenue, New York, New York 10103.*

PRINTED IN THE UNITED STATES OF AMERICA

OPM   9 8 7 6 5 4 3 2

To Christopher James Kaller

CHAPTER 1

BOO!

Jessica Wakefield jumped off the school bus and grabbed her twin sister's hand so they could walk home together. Their older brother, Steven, was walking ahead of them.

"Look at those scary decorations," Jessica said, pointing to a house on the corner. Ghosts made from pillowcases hung from tree branches out front. A cardboard skeleton was taped to the front door, and three pumpkins with faces carved out sat on the porch railing.

Elizabeth pretended to shiver. "I can't wait for Halloween."

"Neither can I," Jessica said.

Elizabeth and Jessica agreed on a lot of things, because they were identical twins. The two girls shared a bedroom. They always split their cookies in half. And they sat next to each other in their second grade class at Sweet Valley Elementary School.

Jessica and Elizabeth looked alike, too. They had blue-green eyes and long blond hair with bangs. When they wore their matching outfits to school, even their best friends couldn't tell them apart.

Jessica and Elizabeth may have looked the same on the outside, but they were very different on the inside. Everyone knew that Elizabeth liked schoolwork, while Jessica couldn't wait for recess. Jessica liked playing space voyagers or jungle safari outside. Elizabeth didn't like to get messy, so she usually played jump rope. But even though they didn't always like the same things or play the same games, Jessica and Elizabeth were best friends.

Now as they looked at the scary decorations, Steven turned around and walked backward. "That's the house where the witch lady lives," he told them. "Every Halloween she comes out and haunts the trick or treaters."

Jessica gulped. "She does?"

"Yes," their brother said, nodding solemnly. "If you go near her house at night she'll get *you*," he added, jumping at them suddenly. Jessica and Elizabeth both screamed in surprise.

"You just made that up to scare us," Elizabeth said.

3

Jessica stuck out her tongue. "That's not funny."

"Got you! Got you!" Steven laughed and ran ahead the rest of the way to their house.

"He was just teasing," Elizabeth told Jessica.

"I know," Jessica said. "He thinks he can do that to us because it's almost Halloween."

The girls reached their front door. "I've got an idea," Jessica said. "Let's try on our costumes from last year."

The girls ran upstairs to their bedroom. Elizabeth opened the door to the large walk-in closet and looked along the shelf. "Here they are," she said, standing on tiptoes to reach higher. She pulled down two clown costumes made of pink polka-dot material. Their mother had sewn wide ruffles around

4

each neck and put yellow pompoms down the front.

Jessica and Elizabeth spread the costumes out on their beds. "Those look like baby costumes," Jessica said. She held hers up in front of herself. It looked too small.

"I think we grew since last year," Elizabeth said.

"We sure did," Jessica said. "They were OK for first grade—"

"But not for second," Elizabeth finished. Each girl often knew what the other one was going to say.

Just then they heard a tapping sound coming from the doorway. Jessica and Elizabeth turned around to see what it was.

"YAAAH!" Steven jumped into their room with a pillowcase over his head. Jessica and

Elizabeth were so surprised that they both jumped.

"Scared you! Scared you!" Steven shouted. He was laughing as he took the pillowcase off.

Jessica threw her clown costume at him. "Quit it!"

"We weren't scared at all," Elizabeth told him.

"Yes you were!" Steven said. "And you look just like a jack-o'-lantern with your front tooth missing."

Quickly, Elizabeth put one hand over her mouth. She had lost a front tooth the week before and felt shy about the gap that showed when she spoke or smiled. "So what?" she said. "Plus I got a special prize from the tooth fairy since it was a front tooth."

Steven laughed and walked out of the twins' room.

Jessica and Elizabeth stood in front of the mirror. The only difference between them was Elizabeth's missing tooth. One of Jessica's front teeth was loose, but it hadn't fallen out yet. Jessica touched it with her finger very gently.

"I can't wait for yours to fall out," Elizabeth teased. "Then we'll be twins again!"

CHAPTER 2

The Pumpkin Vote

Mrs. Otis, the twins' second grade teacher, made an announcement as soon as everyone settled down in their seats on Tuesday morning. "We're going to start the day with a surprise," she said.

Elizabeth looked at Jessica and they smiled at each other. They both knew that the surprise was probably about Halloween. It was all they had been thinking about. They leaned forward eagerly to hear what their teacher had to say.

"As you all know, every class gets to carve

a pumpkin," Mrs. Otis began. "And the class with the best pumpkin will lead the school parade."

"I hope we win," Jessica whispered to Elizabeth.

Elizabeth nodded. Leading the school Halloween parade was an honor. Last year a fifth-grade class had been chosen.

"Let's carve a funny face instead of a scary one," Winston Egbert suggested.

Lila Fowler giggled. "That's easy. We could make it look like you."

Everyone else laughed, even Winston. He was always making silly faces.

"Why don't we take a vote?" asked Mrs. Otis. "Who wants a scary face?"

Elizabeth looked at Jessica. They both shook their heads at the same time. But a few kids raised their hands.

The teacher counted them. "Three," she said. "Now who wants a funny pumpkin face?" Everyone else put their hands up quickly, including Elizabeth and Jessica.

"OK. Funny wins," Mrs. Otis announced. "Now, I want each of you to draw a funny pumpkin face, and we'll vote on which one to use. Who's in charge of art supplies this week?"

"I am," Jessica said. "So is Elizabeth." She jumped out of her seat and ran to the art closet at the back of the room. Elizabeth followed her.

"We'll use plain white drawing paper and regular pencils," Mrs. Otis said. "And let's use the triangle and circle shapes for tracing."

Elizabeth and Jessica gathered all the art supplies and handed them out.

11

"When we have art class," Mrs. Otis continued, "I'll show you how to make bats with black construction paper."

Lois Waller raised her hand. "Can we make ghosts if we want to?"

"Of course you can," Mrs. Otis said. "You can make anything you want."

"I'll make a face that looks like a clown," Elizabeth said as she slid back into her seat.

Jessica was concentrating on making a good outline for her pumpkin face. "That's a good idea. I want to make a clown, too."

"Pssst!"

Elizabeth turned around to see who was whispering to her. It was Todd Wilkins. He held up his design. The mouth was full of teeth with one missing at the front. "It's an Elizabeth pumpkin," he said.

"Ha, ha," Elizabeth said. But she smiled

12

when she turned around again. Todd was always teasing her.

"Mrs. Otis!" Caroline Pearce called out. "Ken's copying my design."

"I am not," Ken Matthews grumbled, but he quickly started erasing his paper.

Elizabeth traced large round eyes on her pumpkin. She drew a round mouth, and then added droopy ears. Jessica glanced over and giggled.

"When you finish your drawings, tape them to the blackboard," Mrs. Otis said. "Then we can all choose our favorite design."

Eva Simpson and Amy Sutton put their drawings up first. Soon, all of the drawings were on the blackboard. Elizabeth didn't think hers was as good as some of the others, especially Todd's. She decided to vote for

13

Todd's, even though it made fun of her a little bit.

"This is a really good one," Lila Fowler said, pointing to Ellen Riteman's. It was a very neat drawing of a grinning pumpkin.

"No way!" Charlie yelled. "I vote for Todd's."

"Me, too," Jerry McAllister said.

Mrs. Otis stood by the bulletin board and pointed to the first design with her pointer. "Any votes for this one?" No hands went up.

One by one, Mrs. Otis pointed to each pumpkin drawing. The most popular ones were Todd's and Ellen's. The class then voted on those two. Todd's got more votes.

"Hooray!" Todd shouted, raising both arms in the air.

"Then this is our official design," Mrs. Otis

said. "We'll carve the pumpkin tomorrow afternoon."

Elizabeth grinned. Halloween was fun. She couldn't wait for trick-or-treating. But she and Jessica still needed costumes. They had to think of something quickly, because Halloween was just a few days away.

CHAPTER 3

Two Good Costumes

When Jessica and Elizabeth got home from school, they told their mother all about the pumpkin contest.

"We voted for the face Todd Wilkins drew," Jessica explained. "It has ears and hair and everything."

Elizabeth took a sip of her milk. "He cut really thin lines for the hair so light will show through. And he drew it with one tooth missing, just like me," she said with a giggle.

"That's very cute," Mrs. Wakefield said. "I know you're excited about Halloween."

"We are," Elizabeth said. "But we still don't have our costumes picked."

Mrs. Wakefield gave them both a big smile. "I'm glad you brought that up. I have a surprise for you two."

"Tell us!" Jessica and Elizabeth shouted at the same time.

Mrs. Wakefield stood up. "I went to a garage sale today, and I found something really special."

"What?" the twins shouted together.

Mrs. Wakefield headed toward the living room. "Let's go take a look."

Jessica and Elizabeth raced through the kitchen door. In the middle of the living room was a cardboard box. Colorful cloth spilled out over the sides.

"Look!" Jessica said. She grabbed a purple and green outfit and held it up.

"A dragon!" Elizabeth exclaimed. "Try it on."

While Jessica put on the dragon suit, Elizabeth found a cowgirl dress with fringe. "I wore an outfit just like this at Wild West Town," she said, remembering the trip she and Jessica had taken with their grandparents.

Jessica began to giggle. "This is too big on me," she said with a laugh. The purple sleeves hung down over her hands. She flapped her arms.

Elizabeth giggled, too. The cowgirl hat didn't fit on her head. "This is way too small."

Mrs. Wakefield pulled out some more clothes. She found a princess dress made of a

sparkly fabric and a black witch's costume. She held them up. "These look like they're just the right size."

"Oh! I want to wear the princess dress," Jessica said. "It's so beautiful." She reached out to touch it.

Elizabeth's eyes widened. She looked disappointed. "I like it, too," she said in a quiet voice.

"But somebody has to be the witch," Jessica pointed out. "Besides, I've always wanted to be a princess."

"Now, now, girls. Talk it over and come to a fair decision," their mother said. "I'll make sure there aren't any rips or broken zippers on these." She left the room with the costumes.

"Let's go upstairs," Elizabeth said, trying to be cheerful again.

21

Jessica nodded. They could decide about the costumes later. Maybe then Elizabeth wouldn't mind letting her have the princess dress, she thought.

When they got upstairs, Jessica sat on her bed. She picked up her stuffed koala to hug. Something black fell off it.

"A spider!" she screamed. She threw the stuffed animal across the room. "Get it away from me!"

Elizabeth leaned over Jessica's bed. "It's only a fake," she said, as she picked up the black rubber spider from the floor.

The girls heard someone laughing. Jessica turned around quickly. "Very funny, Steven!" she shouted.

Steven grinned and ran down the hall to his room. "Happy Halloween!" he yelled.

"I'm going to get him back," Jessica

muttered. She checked the other stuffed animals on her bed for rubber spiders. "If Steven wants a spooky Halloween, he's going to get one!"

23

CHAPTER 4

Class Costumes

Before social studies class began on Wednesday morning, Mrs. Otis stood in front of the room.

"Let's hear what some of you are wearing for Halloween," she said. She looked at Caroline, who sat in the front row. "Caroline?"

"I'm going to be a genie," Caroline said. "With pointy shoes and a veil."

"That's good," Winston said in a loud whisper to Andy Franklin. "That way we won't have to see her face." A few of the kids around him laughed.

Mrs. Otis looked at Winston sternly. "And how about you, Mr. Egbert?"

Winston's face turned red. Then he smiled and stood up. "I'm going to be an alien. Half of me will be green, and the other half will be purple," he said drawing an imaginary line down the middle of his body.

Some of the kids made faces. Jessica wrinkled her nose. It sounded creepy. She would never want to be something so horrible as that.

"I'm going to be the tooth fairy," Lois said. "With fairy wings and a toothbrush for a magic wand."

Elizabeth giggled. "You'll have to visit Jessica pretty soon."

"My tooth won't come out," Jessica said, but she gently wiggled it to see if it was any looser.

Mrs. Otis smiled. "Anybody else?"

"I'm going to be a ghost," Todd announced.

Lila Fowler held up her hand. She always wore fancy costumes that her parents rented from a costume store. "I'm going to be a Mexican lady with a lace shawl and a fan made of real feathers."

Other costumes included a tiger, a boxer, a circus clown, and a ballerina.

Elizabeth hoped Mrs. Otis wouldn't call on her. She and Jessica still hadn't decided who would wear the princess costume. There was even a diamond crown to go with it. Elizabeth wished there were two princess dresses, but she knew there weren't.

"Are you wearing a costume in the parade, Mrs. Otis?" asked Ken Matthews. He was going to be a football player.

Mrs. Otis raised her eyebrows and smiled.

"Yes I am. But it's going to be a surprise." Then she called on Jessica. "What is your costume going to be?"

"A princess," Jessica answered quickly.

Elizabeth stared at her sister. "Jessica!" she whispered. "That's not fair!"

Jessica wriggled around on her chair. "I'm sorry, Liz. I'm so excited about Halloween that the words just came out."

"But we didn't decide yet," Elizabeth reminded her.

"I know," Jessica said. "But I really really really want to be the princess."

Elizabeth didn't get a chance to say any more, because Mrs. Otis began the social studies class.

At recess, Elizabeth stopped Jessica by the swings. "I want to be the princess, too," she said. "Maybe we should flip a coin."

27

Jessica twirled a button on her shirt. "Well, I think that princesses should have perfect smiles," she said. "You can't be a princess if you have a tooth missing."

"That's not fair," Elizabeth said. "Anyway, your front tooth is so loose, it might even come out today."

Jessica put both hands over her mouth. "No it won't," she mumbled through her fingers.

"Let's decide later," Elizabeth said. "OK?"

Jessica nodded, but Elizabeth still felt sad about the problem. How were they ever going to decide?

CHAPTER 5

The Haunted House

"Is everyone finished with dinner?" asked Mr. Wakefield.

Jessica gulped down the last of her milk. "Yes."

"Me, too," said Elizabeth.

"Me, three," Steven said, with his mouth full.

"Good." Their father rubbed his hands together. "Then let's go to the H-a-u-n-t-e-d House," he said in a spooky voice.

Jessica and Elizabeth both pretended to scream. Mrs. Wakefield laughed. She was staying home, but told them to have a good time. Every year the Sweet Valley Community Center organized a haunted house and a Halloween party. It was always fun and always very scary.

"I'll bet you won't even go into the haunted house," Steven said to Elizabeth and Jessica in the car. "Anyone who's scared of rubber spiders is a chicken."

"We weren't scared," Elizabeth said. "The spider just surprised us, that's all."

Steven laughed and made clucking sounds. "Here, chickie, chickie."

"Just you wait," Jessica said. "We'll show you who's chicken."

When they arrived at the Community Center parking lot, Elizabeth, Jessica, and Steven got out of the car and ran to the building. Mr. Wakefield walked quickly to catch up with them. The lobby was decorated to look like a dungeon. Fake spiderwebs hung from the ceiling and the sound of clanking chains and someone groaning could be heard.

"This way," said a teenager dressed like a dungeon guard. He pointed to a dark doorway. Then he let out a creepy laugh. "If you dare!"

Steven was acting brave. "See you chickens on the other side," he said. "*If* you make it." He went to join his friends.

The twins stood at the entrance to the haunted house. "Do you want me to go inside with you?" asked Mr. Wakefield.

Jessica and Elizabeth looked at each other. Their father had always gone with them before. But now that they were in second grade, they wanted to go alone. Elizabeth and Jessica shook their heads.

"OK," Mr. Wakefield said. "I'll see you

later." He turned to join some of the other parents who were waiting in the lobby.

"Are you scared?" Jessica whispered to Elizabeth as they went through the door into a dark hallway.

Elizabeth took Jessica's hand. "Not yet."

"Ewww, yick," Jessica said. Stringy things kept brushing across her face. She crossed her fingers and hoped they weren't real cobwebs. Organ music started playing. Jessica squeezed Elizabeth's hand tight.

"Help!" somebody screamed.

Jessica grabbed Elizabeth. "Are you scared now?" she whispered. It was so dark she could hardly see anything.

Elizabeth gulped. "Not yet."

"Neither am I," Jessica said, her voice quivering.

The two girls crawled into a tunnel. The

sides began to shake and wobble. "Ooo-aah-oooooo!" a voice moaned. Jessica and Elizabeth scrambled through the tunnel as fast as they could. Their hands were sticky from touching the slimy walls. They came to a candle-lit room full of spooky decorations. Someone dressed as a bat was telling a ghost story to a group of visitors. Elizabeth and Jessica stayed to listen. Then they went to the large community room to play Halloween games.

"Look, there's Win bobbing for apples," Elizabeth said.

Jessica laughed. "He's all wet. Just like Todd was when Lois was over and we made applesauce." She was talking about the day Lois had saved Mrs. Brant's kitten from Mrs. Brant's apple tree and she had given the kids a bag filled with apples.

"That was fun," Elizabeth said. Todd, Ken, and Andy were all soaking wet. They were eating a lot of apples, too.

"Hi!" Amy called out to Elizabeth and Jessica. She and Eva ran over to join them. "Did you come through the haunted house yet?"

"Yes. It was really fun," Jessica said. "It was scarier than last year, wasn't it?" Elizabeth smiled. "It was the best ever," she said, looking back at the dungeon.

"Do you want to go through again?" asked Eva.

"Yes!" Amy, Elizabeth, and Jessica said at the same time. They hurried to the dungeon entrance for a second shivery, spooky visit.

CHAPTER 6

Pumpkin Seeds

At home the next day, Jessica, Elizabeth, and Steven were ready to carve the pumpkin.

"Let's make it look like a vampire," Steven suggested.

Jessica nodded. "With long pointy teeth," she added.

"This is the best pumpkin we ever had," Elizabeth said. "It's so round."

Mrs. Wakefield was a good artist. She was studying to be an interior decorator. With a magic marker, she drew a scary face on the pumpkin. "How's that?" she asked.

Elizabeth shivered. "It's good, Mom."

"Yes. Spooky," Jessica agreed.

Mrs. Wakefield carefully cut the top off the pumpkin. Then Elizabeth and Jessica reached inside.

"Yuck!" Jessica made a face. "It's so slimy."

Elizabeth scooped out a handful of seeds. "And stringy."

"We can roast the seeds in the oven," their mother said. "They taste like nuts."

Elizabeth and Jessica and Steven took turns digging out the seeds. "Make sure the inside is nice and smooth," Mrs. Wakefield said, with a smile. "I only work on perfectly clean pumpkins." Then she picked up a sticky pumpkin seed and gently pressed it onto Jessica's forehead.

36

"Jess! You look funny," Elizabeth laughed. She picked up a seed and stuck it on her own cheek.

They all decorated their hands and faces with pumpkin seeds, and everyone laughed at how they looked.

"I can't wait till we go trick-or-treating," Jessica said. A row of seeds across her forehead moved up and down when she spoke.

Mrs. Wakefield turned on the oven to roast the rest of the seeds. "Did you girls decide who's wearing the princess dress?"

Before Elizabeth could answer, Jessica said, "I am."

Elizabeth opened her mouth so wide that some of the seeds on her cheeks fell off. That was the second time Jessica had said she would be the princess.

"Hey, Elizabeth," said Steven. "What's wrong?"

Elizabeth closed her mouth. Another seed fell off her cheek. "I wanted to be the princess, too," she said quietly.

"Yes, but—" Jessica started to say. Her face was pink.

Mrs. Wakefield looked at them. "Did you agree or not?"

Jessica's cheeks got even pinker. "Not yet, but—"

"Girls, how many times have we talked about sharing?" their mother said.

"I'm glad I don't have a twin," Steven spoke up. "I don't have to share with anyone."

Mrs. Wakefield looked at him sternly but didn't say anything.

"Mom, don't you think Elizabeth would

39

make a better witch? She has a missing tooth," Jessica said. "Princesses should have pretty smiles." She smiled to show that she had all her teeth.

Elizabeth stared at the pumpkin. She was angry at her sister. She couldn't help it if her tooth had fallen out.

"Even princesses lose their teeth," Mrs. Wakefield told Jessica.

Jessica frowned. "I know, but—"

"No buts. Both costumes are nice," Mrs. Wakefield said. "One of you will be the princess, and one of you will be the witch. I want you to settle this by tomorrow."

Elizabeth and Jessica both nodded. They *had* to decide by tomorrow. Tomorrow was Halloween!

CHAPTER 7

The Perfect Plan

Jessica woke up first on Halloween morning. She pushed her blanket back and sat up.

Her mouth felt strange. She touched her loose tooth with her finger. "Oh, no!" she gasped. She jumped out of bed and ran to the mirror.

The tooth was so loose it hung crookedly in her mouth. Jessica touched it again, and this time it fell out into her hand. She couldn't believe her eyes.

"What are you doing?" Elizabeth asked as she woke up.

Jessica turned around in surprise. If Elizabeth couldn't be a princess because she had a tooth missing, then Jessica couldn't either.

"Nothing," Jessica said. Her voice sounded strange because she was trying to talk with her mouth shut.

"Why are you talking like that?" Elizabeth asked. She got out of bed.

Jessica turned back toward the mirror. She didn't want Elizabeth to know what had happened.

"Is something wrong?" Elizabeth asked. She walked over to Jessica and stood between her and the mirror.

Jessica didn't answer.

"You're acting very strange," Elizabeth said. "Why won't you open your mouth?"

Jessica pretended to yawn and put her hand over her mouth. "I'm opening my mouth," she said while her teeth were still covered.

"Let me see," Elizabeth said. She grabbed Jessica's hand and pulled it away from her mouth. "Your tooth came out!"

"I know," Jessica grumbled. She held out the tooth to show Elizabeth. "Now we're both missing a front tooth. I guess I can't be a princess, either."

Elizabeth was silent for a moment. "Yes you can," she said. "It doesn't matter about the tooth." She opened the closet. The princess dress and the witch costume were hanging side by side.

"Liz!" Jessica said excitedly. "I have a great idea. One of us can be the princess for the school parade, and then we can switch for trick-or-treating."

"You're right!" Elizabeth smiled. "We can share the costumes."

They were both smiling happily. Now that they each had an empty space in their front teeth, they looked exactly alike again.

"Do you want to be the princess for school or for Halloween?" Elizabeth asked.

Jessica felt good about solving their problem. She stretched her arms high over her head in a ballet pose. "You can be the princess first," she said. "If you want."

"Sure." Elizabeth put on the diamond crown and twirled in front of the mirror in her nightgown.

Instead of dressing in school clothes, Jessica and Elizabeth put on their costumes. Everyone was going to wear their Halloween outfits to school because it was the day of the parade.

"The witch dress is neat," Jessica decided. She made a scary face in the mirror and waved her arms up and down. The sleeves were big, and they flapped like wings.

"Yes," Elizabeth agreed. "You sure look spooky."

Elizabeth had the princess dress on. Jessica thought her sister looked like she had stepped out of a fairy tale. And soon she would look like that, too.

Jessica made another scary face in the mirror. "I can scare a lot of people," she giggled. Then she had another great idea. "You know what?" she whispered to her twin.

"What?"

"I know how we can get back at Steven for trying to scare us," Jessica answered.

Elizabeth's eyes opened wide. She started to smile. "How?"

46

Jessica tiptoed to their bedroom door and peeked out. The hallway was empty. She shut the door and tiptoed back to whisper her plan into Elizabeth's ear. They both started laughing.

Steven was in for a surprise.

CHAPTER 8

The Halloween Parade

Elizabeth and Jessica hurried to class. Animals, clowns, alien creatures, cowboys, racecar drivers, monsters, Raggedy Anns, and many more strange-looking people were walking in the hallways of Sweet Valley Elementary School. Elizabeth didn't know where to look first. It was certainly exciting to be in school on Halloween.

Elizabeth was also happy because her princess dress was so beautiful. The crown made her feel extra special. The best part was that Jessica had figured out how to share it. Elizabeth was glad her twin had thought of the solution. "I wonder what Mrs. Otis is dressed as," she said.

"I don't know. Let's find out," Jessica answered.

When they got to the classroom, everyone else was already in their costumes. But Mrs. Otis was wearing regular clothes.

"I thought you were dressing up," Elizabeth said.

Mrs. Otis smiled. "I will for the parade. But I can't sit down in my costume, so I'll put it on later."

"I wish I knew what it was," Elizabeth said. "I can't even guess."

"Ewww," Jessica said suddenly. She pointed across the room. "Look at Winston."

Elizabeth looked where her sister was pointing. Winston was wearing a costume that was half green and half purple, just as he had said he would.

Caroline was in her genie costume, and she had tiny metal cymbals on her fingers. They went "ping-ping" when she tapped them together. Charlie was a cowboy, and he kept pointing his pretend-gun at kids and yelling "reach for the sky!"

When everyone was sitting down, Todd raised his hand. He was wearing a sheet over his head with holes cut out for eyes. "Where's our pumpkin?" he asked.

"In the cafeteria," said the teacher. "The principal will be judging all the pumpkins just before the parade."

"I hope we win," Jessica said. She pulled the witch hat down on her head so it wouldn't fall off.

Elizabeth nodded. "Me, too."

"Jessica?" Lois piped up. She was dressed as the tooth fairy, and she had a big smile on her face.

Jessica turned around to look at her. "What is it?"

"This is for losing your tooth," Lois said, holding out a bag of sourballs.

Jessica smiled. "Thank you, Lois. I guess I lost my tooth just in time—"

"To meet the tooth fairy," Elizabeth finished for her. "Even I didn't get to do that."

It was hard to wait until lunchtime. Everyone fidgeted in their seats through spelling, math, and social studies class. When the lunch bell finally rang, the whole class shouted, "Hooray!"

Mrs. Otis told them to go to the cafeteria without her. She was going to change into her costume now. When the class got to the lunchroom, the teachers had everyone line up by grade. All the pumpkins were arranged on a table at one end of the cafeteria. Mrs. Armstrong, the principal, was studying each one closely. When she finished looking at the last one, she went back to look at each one again.

"Do you think Mrs. Armstrong will pick ours?" Jessica asked Elizabeth.

"I hope so," Elizabeth said. She held her breath as Mrs. Armstrong stopped to look at their pumpkin for the second time.

"That's ours," Amy whispered to Elizabeth. "She's going to pick us! I just know it!"

Mrs. Armstrong faced the students. "All the pumpkins are excellent. It's always difficult to choose only one winner. But I had to pick one. So, the winner of this year's pumpkin contest is Mrs. Otis's second grade class!"

"Hooray!" Every student in Mrs. Otis's class cheered loudly. Mrs. Armstrong put a blue ribbon on their funny-face pumpkin. The other classes applauded.

Elizabeth and Jessica jumped up and down. "Now we get to lead the parade!" Elizabeth exclaimed.

"Look at Mrs. Otis," Todd shouted. Elizabeth and Jessica both turned around. Mrs. Otis was dressed as a giant chalkboard eraser.

"Now I see why she couldn't sit down," Elizabeth said with a giggle.

"OK, class," Mrs. Otis called. "Line up. The parade is about to begin, and we're right in front."

The paraders walked all the way around the school block. People cheered when they saw the colorful costumes. After the parade, all the classes reassembled in the cafeteria for the costume awards. Mrs. Armstrong, Mr. Butler, who was the gym teacher, and the school nurse were the judges.

"We will award three prizes," Mrs. Armstrong said once she had everyone's attention. "There will be one for the scariest costume, one for the prettiest costume, and a third for the best teacher costume."

Elizabeth twirled in her princess dress. "I hope Mrs. Otis wins," she said.

Jessica crossed her fingers as she walked by the judges. Every student in the school paraded by the three judges. When there were no more costumes to look at, Mrs. Armstrong stood up.

"For the scariest costume, we choose the green and purple alien," she said.

"That's me!" Winston yelled. He ran up to the judges and waved his hands in the air. "That's me!"

Mr. Butler pinned a blue ribbon onto the green half of Winston's costume and shook his hand. Then Mrs. Armstrong awarded the ribbon for the prettiest costume to a fourth grade girl who was dressed as a butterfly.

Finally, Mrs. Armstrong was ready to announce the best teacher costume. She paused for a moment while everyone quieted down. "Mrs. Otis!" she said with a big smile. "As the eraser."

Elizabeth and Jessica both cheered. This was turning into the best Halloween ever!

CHAPTER 9

Scaredy-Cat Steven

"I got you," Steven shouted, waving his plastic laser gun at the twins. "You're vaporized." He was dressed as a space traveler.

"Come on," Jessica said to Elizabeth. "It's time for our plan."

The two girls raced home ahead of Steven. Jessica's witch sleeves flapped in the breeze.

"Chickens," Steven yelled from behind.

"Hurry!" Elizabeth gasped. "He's catching up!"

As soon as they got to the house, Jessica

ran upstairs to Steven's room. They were ready for the first part of their plan. She hid in his closet and shut the door. Elizabeth's job was to stay downstairs and bother Steven so that he would go up to his room.

Jessica tried to breathe without making any noise. A hanger was poking her in the back. She heard the bedroom door open. Steven was coming in.

Jessica put her hand over her mouth to keep from giggling. She heard Steven put something down on his desk. After a few seconds, she scratched on the inside of the closet door. There was silence. She scratched again. Finally, she heard Steven walk toward the closet. Jessica took a deep breath and made her scariest, most horrible face.

The door opened. Jessica jumped out and screamed, "YAAAH!" Steven yelled and

jumped back. He tripped over his own feet and fell onto his bed.

"Got you," Jessica said, laughing.

Steven closed his eyes and opened them again. "Jessica! You really scared me!"

"Scaredy-cat," Jessica shouted.

"You'd better not ever do that again," Steven warned.

Jessica grinned at her brother and ran out of the room. "I won't, chicken," she called. She ran past Elizabeth, who was standing in the doorway. "And you'd better not scare us again, either," Elizabeth said with a laugh.

As the two girls raced back to their room, Jessica decided that being the witch was even more fun than being the princess.

Lila, Amy, Eva, and Ellen arrived after dinner. They were all going trick-or-treating with the twins. Lila wore her Mexican dress, Amy was a cheerleader, Ellen was a ballerina, and Eva was a bumblebee.

"Let's go upstairs," Elizabeth said, leading the way. "Jess and I have to do something."

Lila looked curious. "What? Is it a secret?"

"We have to switch costumes," Jessica explained. "But don't tell Steven."

The girls shut the bedroom door behind them, and Elizabeth took off the princess dress. "We both wanted to be the princess," she began.

"And we both wanted to be the witch," Jessica finished. She and Elizabeth laughed. "But now we have a special plan."

In a whisper, Jessica told their friends about the rest of their plan. Each twin would scare Steven by taking turns as the witch. The others all thought it was a clever idea.

"Did you really scare him this afternoon?" Amy asked.

Jessica nodded. "You should have seen him." She imitated the way he had fallen over in fright.

"Everybody ready?" called Mrs. Wakefield from downstairs. "It's time for trick-or-treating!"

CHAPTER 10

Trick or Treat!

Mrs. Wakefield was dressed in one of Mr. Wakefield's business suits, and she had drawn a mustache on her upper lip. She had a flashlight in one hand. "Is everyone ready?" she asked.

"Ready!" Elizabeth said.

"Do you all have your trick or treat bags?" Mrs. Wakefield asked.

"Yes!" everyone shouted.

"OK, troops, forward, march!" Their

mother opened the door and they all headed outside.

There were already lots of trick or treaters in the street. All the houses had glowing pumpkins out front or in the windows. Elizabeth looked back at their own pumpkin and smiled.

"Let's go to the Brants' house first," Jessica said, running ahead. Mrs. Brant had a beautiful apple tree in her yard.

Elizabeth rang the Brants' doorbell. "Trick or treat!" they all yelled when the door opened.

Mrs. Brant looked surprised. "I've never seen such marvelous costumes!" she exclaimed. "You all look wonderful." She put handfuls of shiny red apples into their bags. "Thank you," Eva said.

"Here come some boys from our class," Eva whispered when they were back on the sidewalk.

Todd, Winston, and Ken were running down the street toward them. They were carrying cans in their hands.

"What is that?" Ellen asked them.

Todd held up his can. It was whipped cream. "In case we need to trick anyone," he explained. He shook the can and pointed it at Jessica. "Watch out, Elizabeth!"

"I'm not Elizabeth!" Jessica screamed. "Don't mess up my princess dress."

Todd looked puzzled. "Jessica? Weren't you wearing the witch costume at school today?"

"Yes!" Jessica said. "It's our witch switch." Jessica and Elizabeth giggled and Todd shrugged, "I don't get it," he said.

The boys looked at each other, and then ran down the street.

"Let's keep going," Mrs. Wakefield said with a laugh.

"Did you see what he almost did to me?" Jessica asked.

Mrs. Wakefield smiled. "I think he was trying to get Elizabeth," she said.

The group stopped at all the houses on both sides of their street. Older boys and girls were starting to go trick-or-treating, too. It was almost eight o'clock when the group started for home. Their bags were full.

"Look. There's Steven," Jessica said, pointing across the street.

Mrs. Wakefield nodded. "He'll be home by eight-thirty. How about going inside and making popcorn? And I'll call Ellen's and Lila's mothers so they can come and pick them up."

Elizabeth held up the front of her long black witch dress as she went in the front door. In just a few minutes it would be her turn to scare Steven. She couldn't wait.

At eight-thirty, Elizabeth went outside again and hid behind a bush. It was very dark. When she peeked out, she saw her brother running up the sidewalk. He came toward the door.

"YAAAH!" Elizabeth screamed as she jumped in front of Steven.

Steven dropped his bag of candy. "Jessica! You promised you wouldn't do that again."

Elizabeth laughed. "Jessica promised, but

I didn't. Can't you tell one sister from the other?"

Steven stared at her. "Elizabeth? You were the princess before."

"Not anymore." Elizabeth hugged him. "I'm sorry, Steven, but you can't call us chicken anymore."

"You didn't really scare me, you know," Steven said. He bent down to pick up the candy that had fallen out of his bag.

Elizabeth laughed again and went inside.

"Did you get him?" asked Jessica.

"I sure did." Elizabeth smiled at her twin. She was glad they had shared the costumes. "This was the best Halloween ever."

On Monday, Mrs. Otis asked the class if they'd eaten a lot of candy over the weekend.

"I ate a lot of chocolate," Elizabeth said.

"So did I," Lila added.

Todd's hand shot up. "My bag was so full that it broke just as I got home," he said. "And my costume was covered with whipped cream."

"I guess you did some tricking along with your treating," Mrs. Otis said with a smile. Everyone laughed. "Halloween is over," Mrs. Otis went on, "but there's a big holiday coming up soon. Does anyone know what it is?"

"Thanksgiving," shouted Winston.

"That's right. And I want you to try out for the school Thanksgiving play," Mrs. Otis announced. "There will be many parts, both big and small."

"I want a big part," Jessica said.

Winston turned around. "You can be the

turkey," he teased, flapping his arms. "Gobble, gobble."

Elizabeth couldn't help laughing with the rest of the class. But Jessica stuck her tongue out at Winston. "You're too goofy to get a part," she said. "Just you wait and see."

Will Winston get even a small part in the Thanksgiving play? Find out in Sweet Valley Kids #13, **STARRING WINSTON EGBERT.**